HAWKINS' HEROES

CAULDRON OF FIRE

TODD MCLEOD & ERIC MEYER

Copyright © 2018 Todd McLeod & Eric Meyer

Swordworks Books

All rights reserved.

Chapter One

"The target village is named Balagor," Intelligence Major Elliot McNally intoned. He was a shortish man, slim, and with a slight stoop. Like a legal eagle trying to make a name for himself as a warrior. He was earnest enough, but that didn't mean he'd get it right. No slip-ups when they attacked another testament to Afghanistan's crumbling infrastructure. No sending men to their deaths. Balagor was a place they'd never heard of, and Hawkins suspected they'd probably be more than satisfied if they never heard the name Balagor again.

The Major paused and looked at the twelve men in front of him. Charlie Platoon, Hawkins' outfit, under the command of Second Lieutenant Tony Lopez. He was a good guy, and he listened when his more experienced NCOs offered advice. Eddie Hawkins sat at the back of the briefing room, knowing he had no involvement in this high-level planning stuff. He was a nobody, a recent recruit, an Average Joe at five feet nine inches, with flaming ginger hair, an abundance of freckles, and clear green eyes.

Hawkins was the gunner in Sergeant Dan Jones' Humvee. His place was up in the cupola, behind the .50 caliber Browning machine gun. His job was straightforward, to keep his keen eyes peeled for any sign of the enemy. And hit them hard before they had a chance to hit them first. After a shaky start in country, he'd got the knack of aiming and firing the heavy weapon, acquiring a reputation as an ace shooter. He had another reputation as an ace shooter, and this reputation was worldwide. Call of Duty, the game he spent most of his off-duty time playing on a Dell eleven-inch laptop he'd recently acquired. Okay, it wasn't an Xbox, but you couldn't lug an Xbox into the field. The laptop was the next best thing.

"You're wondering about this place, and why it's so important," the Major continued, "Our intelligence assessment is they're about to hold a high-level meeting between the Taliban regional commanders and several ISIS commanders who recently arrived in Afghanistan. They're planning to link up to hit a number of strategic objectives. Some are in Kabul, the capital, and these combined attacks are bad news. I don't need to tell you we have enough problems here with the Taliban, and our guys in Iraq and Syria with ISIS. If they link up, God help us all. A Taliban ISIS axis puts us into a whole new ball game.

Sergeant Jones put up a hand. "Major, why don't we just bomb this place if we know they're gonna be there? Drop a few thousand pounds of iron bombs, or hit them with Hellfire missiles, and they'll never know what hit them."

He nodded and smiled. "I see where you're coming from, Sergeant, and believe me, we've considered a bombing mission. You're right; they'd never know what hit them. But the problem is we'd never know who we hit, and we need to know we got them all. This is a onetime opportunity, and that means we have to go in on the ground, identify the enemy, and take them out. Just like SEAL Team Six did with Osama. Eyeball the bastards, and make sure we're taking out the right people. If we offload several thousand pounds of bombs on that place, we could be dropping them on the heads of a few local women stirring the pot for the evening meal. No, this has to be up close and personal. Go in, hit the bastards hard, and leave nothing behind except bodies."

"We'll be going in blind," Lieutenant Lopez said, "We don't know anything about this place. At night there's a lot of room for mistakes."

McNally looked smug. "You're right, Lieutenant, if we went in blind it could be a major screw up. That's why we've prepared a dummy village for you to stage a practice attack. The layout is almost identical to Balagor, and we've dressed up one of our units as insurgents, so you'll encounter a real enemy, or as real as we can make it. This'll be a practice run to be sure when you do it for real you get it right. Don't forget, this isn't for real, so you'll be loaded with blank rounds."

"Is that a good idea?" Sergeant Dan Jones piped up. He was no fool, a tough, leathery vet, working toward the end of his second tour. Tall, a commanding NCO, with piercing blue eyes that can at times be wintry, and at times mysterious, goes by the nickname of Sergeant Dan. He rarely smiles, just does his job, at which he is damn good. The kind of guy a man would feel good about having on his side when the fighting starts.

"After all, that area is still Taliban central, and even though you've prepared this dummy village, we could still run into trouble at any time."

He paused for a few moments. "I see your point, and you're right. No sane man goes unarmed in this country. Okay, you'll load blanks when you go in, but you'll carry live bullets in your spare magazines. Just in case."

The men nodded to each other. Venturing anywhere in Afghanistan, and especially at night, without a good supply of bullets, real live bullets could be a fast way to commit suicide. The Major ended the briefing by handing out maps of the objective to each of the crews. The meeting dispersed, and they left the briefing room. The driver, Winston Bellows, a man who could make a Humvee dance the tango if he so pleased, glanced at him. He was an ace driver, and his dark eyes would squint at every inch of terrain, always choosing the best route. He was one tough hombre with a gangsta past as a getaway driver which he was trying to live down. But still, men counted him the best driver in the Division.

"This looks like a piece of cake, Eddie. You won't need to use that Browning, you can sit in that cupola and play video games."

Hawkins smiled. Gaming had played a large part in his life, but now the Army was his number one priority. Gaming was cool, but this was different, and he'd be careful. Men messed up all the time.

This may be an exercise, but I'll make damn sure I carry plenty of live rounds for the Browning.

He returned to their hut and scanned through a new gaming mag. There was nothing new, and he fired up his phone, connected to the net, and browsed the sites for the latest news, but nothing had changed. He checked the news every day to see what's going on in the gaming world. New mods, new patches, new games. Keeping up was important. But not life or death, not like fighting in Afghanistan.

The following morning they roused them before dawn, and after a hurried breakfast, they climbed into their vehicles. The target village lay ninety-five klicks from Bagram, heading north. North toward enemy territory, and the Intel Major was there to see them off. "I wish you luck, men. Any last questions before you leave?"

Eddie strolled toward him. "Sir, this place, Balagor. I mean; I know it's a mockup of the real target village, but don't you think it's mighty close to enemy territory. If they're watching, they could smell a rat."

He shrugged. "We've been over this several times, Private. Believe me, there aren't any insurgents inside a fifty-kilometer radius. And our own men will be there, although they'll be dressed like insurgents. Relax; it'll go like clockwork. You know what to do, drive in, and give them hell. Just blank rounds, and if it all goes well, we'll debrief you when you get back, and we can fix up for the real thing in the genuine village of Balagor."

"When does this meeting take place, Sir?"

"In five days. It may even be sooner. It's always possible things may change. We have a man on the inside, so we'll know about it. But for now, that's the timescale we're working on, five days."

He thanked him; they swapped salutes, and climbed into their vehicles. Lieutenant Lopez led the column, and Sergeant Dan's Humvee fell second in line. It was late afternoon when they reached the outskirts of the village, and everything was quiet.

The Lieutenant's voice came over the radio. "This is it, lock and load. Don't forget, dummy rounds. We drive straight into this building where they'll be having their cozy heart-to-heart, storm through the door before they realize we're even there, and take them all out. Hit them with everything we have, and they have referees watching, to keep score. Let's make sure we're on the winning side."

"Copy that," Eddie replied automatically, along with a chorus of acknowledgements from the other men. They drove in, their driver skidded to a halt outside the building marked on their maps, and they leapt out of the jeeps. Eddie stayed in place in the cupola. His job was to keep his eyes and ears open for any sign of trouble. For pretend trouble, he reminded himself. At least up here he was alone with his thoughts.

He couldn't explain the feeling, not to himself, or anyone else. But deep down, he knew this mission had all the signs of a first-rate screw up.

Chapter Two

The first sign of the enemy came when a man came out of a building opposite, and he shouldn't have been there. Eddie decided they'd planted several surprises for them to make sure they were on their toes, and he rotated the turret and took aim. Bullets roared out of his Browning, and the stink of bone powder assaulted his nostrils. The man kept coming toward him, ignoring the fuselage, and that was strange. One man walking out in the open, and he should have known he'd have been dead and falling to the ground. Yet he didn't fall to the ground. Instead, he raised his assault rifle, aimed at the jeep, and squeezed the trigger.

The 'clang' of the bullets striking the armored cupola was loud, and Eddie took aim again, searching for a target to return fire. Except he was loaded with blanks, and the guy who'd fired at them was using live rounds. Something was wrong. Badly wrong, and after a moment's hesitation, he ripped out the belt of blanks and loaded a magazine of live .50 caliber rounds. He didn't know why that guy fired at him, but he assumed he was a real enemy who'd slipped into the village unnoticed.

He saw friendlies racing out of the building, and two went down, hit from behind. The truth hit him like a hammer blow. They'd entered a real enemy village, and while he was trying to work out who was the enemy, a group of men came racing from around the side of the building. They were hostiles, Taliban, no question, and on an intercept course for the Americans who'd exited the front doors. He swiveled the Browning, and he still wasn't one hundred percent sure if they were real enemies or their own people. He wasn't sure of anything, only that he had to do something.

In the end, he compromised and fired a short burst over their heads. If they were their own men, they'd return fire with blanks. If they were real insurgents, the bullets would impact on his cupola, and he'd know.

The men dressed as insurgents stopped when his bullets punched the air over their heads. Several went down on one knee, brought their assault rifles up to their shoulders, and a storm of lead flattened against the side of the cupola.

It was enough to convince him he'd made the right guess. He shifted his aim and pulled the trigger.

* * *

Second Lieutenant Lopez was puzzled. They weren't supposed to be using live rounds, and yet the bullets that punched into the side of the building, and the meaty sounds of lead striking flesh, were enough to convince him something was wrong. He swung around to Jones. "Sergeant, something is wrong. They're not supposed to be using live ammunition. We need to get out of here and back into the vehicles. I'll call in, and get them to cease fire."

Dan Jones nodded and waited while Lopez led them out through the door, straight into a hurricane of gunfire. Jones glanced at his crew, Bellows, the driver and Corporal Taylor, the communications man. Another second tour vet, with a past he was trying to live down. Always checking and double-checking everything, as if scared he was about to repeat a mistake he'd made before he joined the unit.

"They're shooting at our men. Lock and load, live rounds, we're going out shooting."

They burst through the door in a wedge formation, Jones in the center, and one man either side. Lopez was wounded, and two more of his men were down. Jones turned to Taylor and Bellows. "Get the casualties into the jeeps. We're getting out here. Move it."

He raced over to Lopez. "Lt, how bad is it?"

The Lieutenant was clutching his shoulder, trying to stop the bleeding, and he looked at Jones. "Bad enough. Take charge of the platoon, and get them out of here."

"I'm on it, Lt. Hang in there."

He rounded up the survivors, and they retreated to the jeeps, returning fire at an enemy they'd barely seen. All they could do was fire at the muzzle flashes, and by expending ammunition at a furious rate; they managed to extricate themselves. They drove away with half the men either dead or injured. He'd radioed ahead, and when they drove through the gates, medics were waiting for them with gurneys and orderlies to carry them into the base hospital. Major McNally, the intelligence officer, called Sergeant Jones over.

"You're the most senior rank to survive that debacle, what happened?"

"What happened was the biggest fuck up I've ever known in this man's army. Those pretend Taliban were real Taliban. I don't know what happened to our guys, but they weren't there. Just Talibs, and they weren't firing blanks."

The Major grimaced. "It wasn't supposed to happen, Sergeant. All I can conclude is the enemy attacked that village hours before the exercise and killed our men. When you went in, they saw American soldiers and started shooting."

"You're probably right, but it gets worse. To make it more realistic, you put a sign up at the entrance to the village, a sign that said Balagor. They're not stupid, and if they haven't worked it out yet, they soon will, and they'll know what we're planning. An attack on the village of Balagor to kill everyone at that meeting."

He nodded. "I doubt that, Sergeant, but I'll try to find out."

"Maybe. Was there anything else, Sir?"

"No, dismissed."

Dan walked away and joined the rest of his men. Eddie was sitting with his back against the rear wheel, his head in his hands. Al Taylor and Winston Bellows were nearby, smoking and chatting, but he went to Eddie first. "That was a bad one."

"No shit. That was the biggest screw up I've ever seen. I thought intelligence was supposed to have some intelligence. What happened to the idea of communications? Why didn't anyone call it in?"

He shrugged. "I just don't know the answer to that one."

"Someone ought to be shot for getting those men killed."

Jones nodded. "You're right, and it's even worse than you think. They'll hold their meeting elsewhere, and if they make an agreement, we can expect renewed attacks to come thick and fast. You ain't seen nothin' yet."

Eddie was thinking hard. "Sarge, if they're still going to hold this meeting, there must be away to find out where."

"I doubt it. It took them weeks, months of planning to work this one out, and intelligence will've been listening to cellphone intercepts, radio traffic, email communications, you name it. If they're going to meet in the next twenty-four hours, there's no time to find the location."

"The enemy would have the same problem," Eddie said. He went on to explain what he meant, and the more he talked, the more Dan Jones looked interested.

"We're going back to find that Intel Major. Tell him what you just told me."

They had to drag him out of the mess, where he was drowning his sorrows after the debacle. He met them in the lobby of the officers' mess, and he didn't look happy. He'd been drinking, and his words were slurred. "What is it, man? After tonight's disaster, I don't want to listen to ideas for any more disasters."

"You want to hear this," Jones said, "Go ahead, Eddie."

"Well, Major, it's like this. The intelligence took you weeks to assemble. If the enemy is to hold another meeting, they'll have the same problems of logistics and communications, and it'll take time. Which means they'll be making cellphone calls, radio transmissions, and they'll be moving around the countryside to get people together. What we need is for your electronic warfare people to carry out an intensive analysis of signals over the past few hours, and the next few hours. In the meantime, we could go back into that area and find a prisoner. Any one of them, Taliban or Isis, is bound to know what they planned. It has to be soon. These people would have come from all over, Afghanistan, Pakistan, Syria; you name it. And they'll be itching to get back before we get onto them."

He nodded slowly. "It's possible, just possible. But who would be crazy enough to go back in after what happened?"

Eddie looked at Dan, who replied, "I'm up for it, Major."

"You, Sergeant."

"Me and my crew. They killed good men tonight, and we all want payback. Besides, if we don't stop them, we'll have extremist lunatics pouring into the country from all over the world. We'd be in even deeper shit than we are already."

He paused, thinking. "How would you play it? What's the plan?"

"We'd go back in there, pick up a prisoner, and wring the whereabouts of the new meeting place out of him."

"Just like that?"

"Damn right we would, Sir. They're not getting away with what happened back there."

He sobered quickly as he thought about what they'd said. If that meeting went ahead, it'd be a disaster in the making, a major disaster for the Coalition effort, and a personal disaster for his career.

I should have planned better, allowed for contingencies, and I failed. These men, the veteran sergeant and the young private soldier, is their suggestion a workable plan, or another step into disaster?

He took no more than a minute to see the merits of what they said. Failure meant they'd kill a few more Talibs, and die themselves, most probably. At least it'd be a hero's death. Success would put everything right, for him, and for every American soldier inside Afghanistan.

"Okay, we'll do it."

"We, Sir?"

"I said we. I'm going with you, Sergeant. Get your platoon ready, gas up the Humvees, and we'll teach those bastards not to play games with us. Thirty minutes, no more. I'll see you in the vehicle park."

"It's gonna be hairy out there, Major," Dan warned him, "They won't be throwing paper clips at us."

He grimaced. "That's what you think of us intel guys, is it?"

Dan reddened. "Well, uh, no, Sir."

"It's okay, maybe we deserve it. Thirty minutes."

Chapter Three

He stared down at the bodies strewn over the village, an older man with wisps of gray hair sticking out from underneath his brown turban. He wore the traditional robes of a Mullah, and he was the spiritual leader of the various Taliban units scattered around this region.

"What were they after, and what were they doing here? I don't understand. Some of them are dressed in Afghan robes, why would they do that?"

The other man, the commander of the local insurgent group centered on Balagor, shrugged. "I've no idea, I don't get it. Did they plan to infiltrate one of our groups?"

Mullah Akbari scoffed.

"In this way? Coming in here with Coalition vehicles, jeeps with mounted machine guns, and soldiers in uniform? No, that isn't the answer. There must be something else."

At that moment, a young fighter rushed up, and he was holding a thin sheet of plywood. He held it up for them to see. "Look, someone's put up a sign on the village, but they've made a mistake. It says Balagor, but our village is ten kilometers from here."

The two older men studied the board with interest. Sure enough, it was roughly painted and in two languages, Pashto and English. "Are you sure the Americans put up the sign?"

He looked bewildered. "Mullah Akbari, who else could it have been? The last time we were here, there was no sign. Yet after the Americans came, the sign was here. It's almost like they wanted to pretend this was Balagor."

"An easy mistake to make," Commander Aziz murmured, his cruel face looking puzzled. His cheek bore the scar of a bullet wound that had sliced across his face from side to side, gouging a furrow in his nose, so it looked like a separate appendage. "Why else would they put up the sign? There's no reason for it."

Mullah Hamza Akbari shook his head, and the dawning of realization was in his cold, dark eyes, his brow furrowed in thought. "I believe there is a reason. They wanted to pretend this village was Balagor. It is because of the meeting we have planned. They found out about it, and they intend to attack."

The Commander stared at him. "Meeting? Which meeting?"

He waved away as if it was of no consequence. "You were to be told in good time, but until then the object was to keep it a secret. Somehow, they've found out."

He went on to explain the importance of it, and how they were bringing Islamist leaders in from different parts of Asia and from the Middle East.

"We plan to join forces and launch a mass attack on the Coalition. We will drive them from this Islamic Paradise, and this time we'll hit them so hard, they'll keep running until they've crossed the borders, and they never come back."

The other men's eyes glowed with fanatical interest. "This is really true? We can drive the infidels from our country?"

"We can drive them from every Islamic nation where they have dared to interfere. Believe me, their days are numbered. But first, we need to warn our people."

"We'll have to find a new meeting place," the Commander nodded.

"Negative, it's not possible. We've made all the arrangements for security, and we have hundreds of fighters coming in from all over the country to protect this meeting."

"But, they have aircraft, how can we stop them?"

A look of cunning came into his eyes. "What they don't know is the meeting is not planned to take place inside the village, but in a cave complex three kilometers to the east. We will put enough fighters in place to make them think they have scored a victory, but it will be a very costly victory. When they attack, we will hit them from all sides. Of course, they have aircraft as you say, and ultimately we can't beat them. But we will kill scores the soldiers, perhaps hundreds. A huge victory, and meanwhile, our leaders can conduct their meeting safe in the knowledge their location is unknown to the enemy."

The Commander grinned. "We cannot fail, Mullah. This will be a tremendous victory, the beginning of the end for the Americans."

He nodded. "You're correct, this will be the beginning of the end. Now, we have to start making arrangements for the ambush. I believe the Americans call it 'bushwhack', and that's exactly what we'll do. We'll bushwhack the soldiers when they come in, and most will never leave." His expression formed a gloating smile, "Except in body bags."

* * *

They were driving in a convoy of four vehicles, with Sergeant Jones' Humvee leading. Major McNally was riding in back along with Corporal Al Taylor, their communications man. Up in the cupola, Eddie was thinking, and he was thinking hard. He remembered driving into that village, and amidst the confusion, the gun flashes and bullets sitting all around them, he recalled seeing the sign they'd erected to try to make the exercise more realistic. The name in Pashto and English stated the name of the village was Balagor. Of course, it wasn't Balagor. That was the target they plan to hit after a successful trial run on the dummy village. Except they left in a hurry, and the Taliban were in control. Were they stupid? Definitely not. In the guise of the Mujahideen, they'd kicked out the Soviets, and when many of the diehard Islamists morphed into the Taliban, they'd taken control of Afghanistan and formed a government.

He didn't need to ask himself whether they'd work it out.

They'll work it out, no question, but somehow, Major McNally hasn't got his head around it. Damn, he wouldn't get very far playing Call of Duty, if he can't spot a simple trap like that without falling into it.

He leaned down so they could hear him. "Major, Sir, I wondered about that sign in the village."

"Sign? Which sign?"

He explained about the sign he'd seen, stating the name of the place was Balagor. "The thing is, they'll know exactly what we're planning. That we know the name of the location of their meeting, and that this was just a dummy run. All I'm saying, Sir, is they'll waiting for us."

He stared back at Hawkins, and he looked unsure. "Let me think about this for a few moments. Sergeant Jones, how far are we from the dummy village?"

"We'll be there in around ten minutes, Major. Say around three kilometers."

He acknowledged but didn't say anything. Winston Bellows drove carefully, not making too much noise, and showing no lights. He didn't want to drive them off a cliff or into a ravine. The journey took longer than Jones had estimated, but eventually Bellows slowed.

"About one klick and we'll be driving into the village. What do you want me to do?"

"I'm trying to work it out." He tossed Bellows an irritated glance and then seemed to come to a conclusion, "My assessment is they won't have worked it out. These are primitive peasants, and I doubt most of them can read."

Hawkins was listening in the cupola, and he couldn't believe what he was hearing.

If they can't read, why would they bother to put signs outside their villages?

"That's just guesswork, Major. It only takes one man who can read, and they could work it all out."

McNally gave him a superior gaze. "That's most of what we do in intelligence, guesswork. It's the way we work, fragments of information, and balance of probabilities to form our assessments. I don't think we have anything to worry about. We should go in there, and they're sure to have left at least a couple of their people to keep an eye out, in case we come back. But they'll be expecting us to come back in force, not just a platoon. So we'll carry on as planned, and sneak in through the back door. Do our best to capture an insurgent, and pump him for information."

Jones didn't reply, but Bellows heard the order, and he drove forward, slowly, as if he was waiting for someone to countermand. In the end, Hawkins couldn't help himself. "Major, you're gambling everything on them not being able to read. What if they can read? We'll be screwed."

"You give them too much credit, Private Hawkins. Just do your job, and watch out for hostiles. We're going in."

Al Taylor relayed the order to the other three jeeps. They increased speed, and minutes later they were in the center of the village. Everything was quiet, no one moving through the darkness, and even the bodies had disappeared. McNally was look around, staring at each stone cottage in turn, as if he could see through solid stone and work out if anyone was inside. Eventually, he gave up.

"The place is empty. We'll stop here and search the cottages. We may find something that will help us find out if they've worked out what we're planning."

Hawkins shook his head in despair.

Major they've worked it out, and they're getting ready to give us a hot welcome.

He stayed behind the Browning as men searched each cottage in turn, and they found nothing. He began to relax, and his eyes roamed around the gloom, looking for anything. Anything out of the ordinary, a threat to the men he was supposed to protect, and he found nothing. Almost nothing. Something moved a fraction about two hundred meters away.

An animal, a bird, or a human being?

He sighted along the barrel, using the AN/PVS-20 Starlight scope, and gradually it became clear. What he'd seen wasn't movement, but a reflection as the beam of a flashlight hit metal.

The faintest glow, almost none, but he could make out the shape of a man. A man holding a weapon, and now it moved, a long barrel eased out from behind the stone wall of a well. It was an ambush. They'd left at least one man in place just in case they came back. Just like he'd have done if he knew what the Talibs must now know. The question was, how many of them were there? He pressed the transmit button and spoke quietly.

"This is Hawkins in the lead jeep. I see a hostile behind the well, two hundred meters north of my position. Suspect has a machine gun, type unknown."

Jones acknowledged. "Is it just one man?"

"Could me more, Sarge. Watch him while I look around some more."

"Copy that."

He rotated the cupola, inch by inch, quartering every inch of ground, and he spotted them. He was certain he had them all, four men. Each armed with a machine gun, and they were waiting for the moment when they could slice them into thin pastrami. He sang out their positions and returned to the first man he'd seen.

"This is Hawkins. I have the man behind the well covered."

"Copy that. I'll take the man behind the wrecked truck to the west."

Weller, the gunner from the rearmost vehicle, added, "I have the gomer to the south."

"I have the guy up on the roof."

"Copy that. Wait for me to start shooting, and give 'em hell. Thirty seconds."

Several double clicks on the radio acknowledged, and they waited for it to start. And waited.

Chapter Four

Major Elliot McNally, veteran of innumerable meetings and policy planning sessions, wasn't happy. "I don't like this, Sergeant. We don't know who we're shooting at."

"The enemy, Sir."

"That's as maybe, but we came here for a prisoner. We can't take a prisoner if they're all dead. Hold your fire when we go in. I need to evaluate so we can get this right."

Like last time.

Hawkins groaned to himself. The guy could get them all killed, and he wasn't having any of it. To hell with the orders. A moment later he squeezed the trigger.

The long burst of .50 caliber machine gun fire tore through the wall surrounding the well, and the bullets ripped into the guy hiding behind the well. A moment later, the rest of the jeeps opened fire, and the night was torn apart by heavy fire. Inside of the first minute, they'd hit all four targets, and slowly, the gunfire petered out. There was just the noise of Intelligence Major Elliot McNally shouting at them to cease fire, which they did because there was nothing left to shoot.

"Dammit, I told you to hold your fire. They're all dead."

And we're alive. Best not say it aloud. McNally might take it the wrong way.

Eddie glanced through the Starlight scope and worked it around the village. Looking for something, anything, a Talib they might have missed.

Dammit, there's a guy, hiding in the shadows.

"Sergeant Dan, there's a live one. Five o'clock, he's crouched in a doorway."

"Is he aiming a weapon?"

"Uh, no, I don't think so."

"Gimme that scope," McNally shouted. Hawkins squeezed out of the cupola and let him go ahead, "Yeah, I see him. Men, good news, we may have a prisoner. Sergeant Jones, get out there and secure him."

"Yessir."

Dan spoke quietly on the radio, and another Humvee backed away to circle around the dwelling. Minutes later, he got the message he was waiting for. "We're in position."

"Copy that. If he tries to run, grab him. Eddie, I'm going out there with Bellows. Cover us."

"Copy that."

He waited and watched. Dan and Winston strolled along in the center of the track that ran through the middle of the houses, as if they were going for a Sunday afternoon stroll. At the last moment, as they were passing the target, they split up and ran at him, one either side. Seconds later they dragged him back. They had a prisoner, and Hawkins climbed out to look at him. Jones tossed him the guy's AK-47. He played his flashlight over the mechanism and looked inside the barrel. It was coated with rust, and if it fired, it'd likely do more damage to the shooter than his intended target.

He switched his gaze to the prisoner. He was young, little more than fourteen-years-of-age. He looked thin, to the point of emaciation, and his clothes were little better than rags. Whatever else they were doing, they weren't living high on the hog. He wondered what he'd been up to with a rifle that'd only be useful if he reversed it and used it like a club.

"I'll handle this," McNally said, pushing them aside. He faced the kid and smiled.

"Do you speak English?"

He didn't reply, and the Major looked disappointed. "That's it. We don't have an interpreter. We'll have to take him back with us."

They looked at each other, and Dan told him how it worked in these parts. "Sir, they always say they don't speak English. Let me try."

He waved a hand. "Go ahead. I'm gonna take a look around, see if there's anything useful we can use."

He disappeared into the nearest hut, and Dan tried a few questions, without any response. He shrugged. "I guess he really doesn't speak any English. We have to know if they've worked out our real target is Balagor, or have they moved the meeting elsewhere. By the time we get back, and the Afghans get the truth out of him, it could be too late."

Eddie regarded the kid, and he didn't look much different to the way he'd looked four years before, when he was fourteen; fresh-faced, a bit naïve, but with his life in front of him. If the Afghans got their hands on him, they'd tear him apart.

"Sarge, I have an idea. Let me try."

A shrug. "Knock yourself out, Eddie."

Hawkins took the laptop out of its protective case, the Dell with the Intel i7 quadcore chip, SSD hard drive, and sixteen-gig memory. Most important was the software, Call of Duty. He booted the machine, loaded the game, and walked out to the kid, who was sitting on the ground, covered by Winston's M4A1.

He showed him the screen, and the dark eyes looked at it with interest.

"You ever seen anything like this? It's a game, Call of Duty. A combat game, and it beats the hell out of the real thing."

The boy was mesmerized. "It does?"

Eddie suppressed a smile.

So he does speak English.

"Oh, yeah, watch this."

He spent five minutes playing a level he'd become expert at, and the kid's eyes were like saucers as he watched. "Your guys in Balagor would be better off playing this than sitting out there with loaded assault rifles, waiting for Coalition aircraft to bomb the crap out of them."

He was caught up in the game as Eddie manipulated the trackpad and buttons like the expert he was. So caught up, he spoke without thinking. "They're not in Balagor. It won't be a problem."

He kept on playing. "How come it won't be a problem?" The kid didn't answer, and he made a fancy move, destroying a platoon of enemy armor, "I mean, when those missiles hit, they'll be toast."

"No, they're outside Balagor. Inside a cave system, three kilometers due east, so they'll be safe."

"Uh, huh, that's good. You want to try this?"

"Yes."

He grabbed the laptop like it was food for a starving man, and Eddie showed him how it all worked. He couldn't take his eyes off the screen, so Hawkins left him guarded by Bellows, and went to find Dan.

"I got him to talk."

The Major appeared from behind the Humvee, and he rushed up. "What was that? Did you say he talked?"

Eddie explained what he'd said, and McNally's eyes gleamed. "A cave system three klicks due east? You did well, Private. Secure the prisoner. We're leaving."

"We're going back?"

"The hell with going back. We'll go forward and conduct a reconnaissance, find out what's going down. Then we report back. We need to do this right."

Dan coughed. "Sir, this meeting, if it's tonight, they'll have gone by the time we get there. Shouldn't we radio it in and let them handle it?"

"Absolutely not. We could send our planes to bomb an empty area, or send more men into an enemy ambush. No, we carry out a recon first, then we call it in. Mount up."

They drove on through the dark night, and Major McNally spent time checking and rechecking his calculations on the electronic tactical pad. From time to time, he'd ask questions to confirm his estimates, and each time, Sergeant Dan responded with as few words as possible. Bellows was driving with night vision goggles, like two alien eyes sprouting out of his face, but it meant they could manage without lights that would have alerted the enemy.

"Something coming up ahead. Looks like buildings."

"Just as I thought. Turn off the track and head east."

"Major, it's rough ground, are you sure this is the way?"

"I'm sure. There'll be a hill somewhere in front of us. The terrain will start to slope upward. These caves are about two klicks in front of us. I've plotted it on the map."

Dan interrupted. "Sir, you're taking us awful close. They may not see us, but they'll sure hear us, and they'll have posted guards if this meeting is that important. We could run into heavy enemy fire."

"We'll be fine, Sergeant. Nothing to worry about."

"I'm not worried, Major. I'm trying to be sensible."

"This won't take long. Take it easy, all of you."

To Eddie, watching for hostiles from the cupula, the Major sounded like a dentist who was about to perform a painful extraction, and reassuring his patient it wouldn't hurt a bit.

I trust Dan to know what he's doing. Unlike Major McNally.

He swept his gaze through three hundred and sixty degrees, and everything happened at the same time. The three jeeps, the rest of their platoon, they weren't there.

"Major, we're on our own. We left them behind."

"Hostiles, hostiles," Dan shouted at the same instant as a line of tracer fire arced through out of the night and tore past their jeep. "Winston, take evasive action."

"I'm on it." He was already swinging the wheel over, and where they'd been a second before became a mass of converging machine gun fire, tracers flickering like fireflies. Then the eruption of flame and smoke lit up the sky, as a missile hurtled toward them. Bellows drove like a maniac, twisting and turning, finding every natural obstacle he could put between them and the Taliban. They almost made it, but the front wheels slammed into a deep rut, the Humvee stopped dead, and almost vaulted nose over tail. It came to a stop.

The target was too tempting, and the enemy machine gunners adjusted their aim. The next bursts tore through the vehicle, but they didn't have it all their own way. Hawkins swiveled the Browning around and took aim at the source of the tracers. He fired a long burst, and one machine gun stopped, and then another. He screwed up his gaze, staring through the Starlight scope, and he saw the missile shooter standing up ready to launch the next rocket. A twitch of the gun and he had it lined up. He fired at the same moment as the shooter, and the Talib fell as it was leaving the launch tube. The missile struck the ground, exploding in a crescendo of smoke and fire, and the screams of the men who'd been close were loud in the night air.

"Major, we need to get out of here," Dan shouted, but he didn't get a reply. McNally was slumped in back, and he put his ear close to his face to listen for his breathing. He was still alive, "Major, you were hit, how bad is it?"

The voice was weak. "I can handle it. Corporal Taylor, radio in and tell them we've found the enemy. They're to send in an immediate air strike and bomb this place back into the Stone Age. Sergeant Jones, get us out of here. I need a medevac. I don't feel so good."

"I heard that," Al Taylor grunted, "I'm sending the message now with the coordinates."

He started speaking into the headset, having to shout over the noise and the chaos. They'd brought up another machine gun, and bullets were perforating the thin body of the Humvee. At any moment they were going to take more hits. Eddie felt something slam into his armored vest, and a further burst tore into Al Taylor and the radio.

"Dammit, we've lot communication."

"Can you fix it?"

He looked at the Sergeant. "It won't be easy in the middle of a firefight, but I'll do my best."

"Okay, Winston, we need to get out of here."

"You're not kidding." He applied power, and the Humvee rocked backward and forward, but the front wheels were stuck, "It's not happening, Sarge. We won't get out of were without a tow, and the rest of our guys are back there somewhere."

"No chance of digging us out?"

"It's rocky ground," he murmured.

"Right." He took a last look around, "We're screwed."

Chapter Five

Dan ducked as a long burst of machine gun fire tore through the interior and gave the only order possible. "Get out, everybody. Al, bring the radio, and see if you can fix it later. Winston, help me with the Major. Eddie, unhook the machine gun and bring it along."

"What about the kid?"

"Kid?"

"The Taliban prisoner."

"Yeah, we'll have to take him with us. Do what you can."

Eddie unmounted the Browning and staggered under the weight of eighty-eight pounds. He looked at the spare belts of ammunition and knew he wouldn't make it. Then there was the boy, who looked up at him terrified. Maybe he thought he was about to kill him. Probably because that's what his people would do. He had an idea, but first things first, and he tucked his laptop into his pack and shouldered it. The boy was watching him, or rather watching what he'd done with the key that opened the door to Call of Duty.

He looked at him. "What's your name?"

A pause. "Ahmad."

"Uh, huh, my name's Eddie. Say, we're in a lot of trouble here, and we need your help."

The eyebrows narrowed with suspicion. "Why should I help you, Eddie?"

"Why, because if we stay here, we'll all die, and that includes you as well as this man, the Major, who's wounded. How about it? Do you have a Mom and Pop waiting for you?"

"Yes, they are waiting for me to send them money for food."

"Help us get out of here, and you'll see them again. Otherwise, we all die here. All I'm asking is you help me to carry the Browning and the ammunition."

"You are my enemy. This would be wrong."

"No, we're not your enemy. The guys you think are your friends are the enemy. Afghanistan was a decent country before the Taliban. It could be decent again. Help us, and help a wounded man live."

He paused for several seconds, and Dan was shouting at him over the crackle of incoming fire. "Eddie, get the Lt out. Move out now while we're still breathing!"

"On the way." He looked at Ahmad. "What's it gonna be?"

"Can anyone play that game on the computer?"

"Yeah, of course."

"I will help."

Between them they lugged the heavy gun and the ammo belts after Dan and Winston, half carrying the Major, and Taylor with his radio. The ground was littered with places to take cover, provided the enemy didn't know their position. If they fired another RPG rocket, they didn't need to have line of sight. An explosion nearby would fry them.

Al was working frantically on the radio, Winston used his M4 to take potshots every time he saw an enemy turban surface, and Dan was applying a dressing to the Major's wound. Eddie set up the Browning, leaning the barrel against a low parapet of fallen rocks. He showed Ahmad how to load in a fresh belt of ammunition, and the boy seemed to take his change of sides as a done deal.

The boy was looking at his pack, and he smiled. He was wondering when it would be all over, and he could do some more gaming. The poor kid should have been home with his parents, his belly full of food, and his clothes at least patched and repaired. Not out here with heavily armed and armored Coalition soldiers on one side, and the vicious, brutal fighters of the insurgency on the other. "Do you see a target?"

The kid jumped. "Excuse me?"

"A target, something to shoot at." He grinned, "Rack up a few points."

"Ah, yes, a target. There." He pointed at a shadowy place up in the rocks, "Up there, a machine gun."

"I don't see anything."

"It is there."

"Okay."

He sighted at the dark patch of rock and squeezed the trigger. The .50 caliber shells hammered out of the muzzle, tore through the darkness, and hammered into the target area. A chorus of screams came from up there, and he assumed he'd done enough. He glanced around, searching through the Starlight scope for more targets, but everything had gone quiet. A bust of static came from the radio, and he assumed Al had repaired the damage. He spoke into the microphone and called over to Dan.

"They're in the air, and they're asking for coordinates for the strike."

"You have the coordinates, what's the problem?"

"Uh, the problem is they're our coordinates. We're that close, Sarge."

"Damn."

He glanced down at the Major, who raised his head, evidently recovering. "I heard that, Sergeant. We know where they are, so all we have to do is pull back, and they can bomb the crap out of them. Don't forget, this is a reconnaissance mission. The purpose is to find the enemy, report their location, and pull back to let the airstrike finish them. When we're clear of the area, we'll give them the coordinates."

"The delay could give them a chance to get away, Sir."

"I gave you an order, Sergeant."

He gave him a reluctant nod. "If you say so, Major. Okay, everyone, we're pulling back."

Hawkins looked at Ahmad. "We're moving back to the track. Help me with the gun."

"That is a bad idea, Eddie."

"Bad why?"

"Because they are behind us. The Taliban."

"How do you know?"

At first he seemed reluctant to divulge more. But after a hesitation, he explained. "I know because that is the plan to defend this place in case of attack. They positioned a unit of fighters in Balagor, with orders to advance to the track and block any retreat. They were expecting you."

"Yeah, I get that. Sarge, you need to hear this."

He explained what Ahmad had said, and he took it all in. "It makes sense. This has been a crapshoot from the start. Okay, we'll have to move south as far as possible, and call in the strike."

"What was that?"

He looked at the Major. "A problem, Sir. Eddie, tell him what the kid told you."

He explained it to the Major, who was shaking his head almost before he started talking.

"You're saying the Afghan prisoner told you this?"

"Yessir, that's correct."

"Forget it. It's all bullshit. Tactical and strategic decisions can only be made on the basis of sound intelligence data, not on the say-so of some prisoner."

"He wants to help us, Major. He knows what he was doing was wrong."

"I don't care. Forget what he told you. Sergeant Jones, get us moving."

Jones glanced around, clearly uneasy. The incoming fire had eased, and it was almost like they wanted them to move. Eddie glanced around again, and there was nothing. But he trusted what Ahmad had said. It made sense, yet the Major acted like he was deaf.

Why won't he listen? He could be taking us into another ambush, and he's acting like a combat vet, not a desk warrior. Yet he's the man with the senior officer's rank, so we don't have any choice.

As if to herd them the way they wanted them to go, bullets began to spit out from ahead, where they'd be gathering for that meeting. Trying to shoo them away, and if he had any doubts, they disappeared. He tried one last time. "Sarge, this is all wrong. We're walking into a trap."

He shrugged. "Orders is orders, Eddie. Better keep that Browning handy, I have a feeling we're gonna need it."

They started moving west, toward the track, and they made fifty meters before several shots came from behind them. Someone else laying down fire to push them away, but this guy wasn't that good. The bullets came close, too close, and Dan shouted, "Get down, everyone. Eddie, hit those sonsofbitches."

"Copy that, Sarge, and it'll be a pleasure."

He propped the Browning, and with Ahmad already acting like an experienced loader, the two young men started to talk back to the Talibs behind them who'd done the shooting. They spoke in the only language they'd understand, a Morse code of hot lead. No complicated succession of dot, dot, dot, dash, dash, dash. Nothing fancy for the medieval minds trying to kill them. This was much simpler, a series of staccato bellows from the heavy caliber machine gun. Once again, he couldn't see them, and he aimed at the gun flashes.

More screams, so he'd scored some hits, and watching through the Starlight scope, he saw them at last. Leaping up from their hiding places, and they were pissed. In the darkness, they were invisible. Or they should have been. Except through the scope they were laid out like empty beer cans on a fairground shooting range. He fired and worked the muzzle of the Browning along the line of men coming toward them. They realized their mistake, and someone shouted an order. They retreated, ducking back out of sight, and the firing stopped.

They waited, and it'd gone quiet. Winston said, "Whadda we do, Sarge."

"I'm thinking. Major, we..." He stopped and bent down to look at the wounded officer, except he wasn't wounded, not anymore. "He took a bullet. I think he's dead. Wait while I see if he's breathing."

A moment later, he straightened up. "The bullet took him in the heart, right in the center. He's dead."

Dan looked around, clearly unsure of his next move. He glanced at Eddie. "You did well hitting those insurgents. They've stopped firing. At least for now."

"Sarge, the ones who were still alive stopped firing because they're still trying to push us back to the track. They're waiting for us."

"You're sure? You still believe that kid?"

"I do. Sarge, he's young, and he just wants a life, like you and me. He was telling the truth."

He nodded. "That may be so, but there's another problem. If we stay here, they're waiting for the coordinates to launch the missiles, and we're right next to them. They'll be dropping them on our heads."

He stared back at him. "We don't have a choice. We're a few meters away from the biggest gathering of cutthroats and murderers in the known world. If we have a chance to get them, we have to take it." He had an idea, "Call in the location, and we'll have a few minutes before they get here. Let me talk to him."

"Okay. Al, get on the radio, and tell them to start the attack."

"Attack where? Which target coordinates do I give them?"

A pause. "Give them our location, right here. They're to drop on us."

"On us? Are you kidding me?"

"Do it, Al. Do it now, before it's too late."

He signed and nodded. "It's your funeral. Matter of fact, it's all our funerals."

He called it in, and already Eddie was explaining it to Ahmad. "They'll be raining missiles down on this place in the next few minutes, like a cauldron of fire. Ahmad, we need somewhere we can hunker down."

"Hunker down?"

"Hide. Away from the explosions."

His eyes registered understanding. "Where your vehicle stopped, there is a deep fissure in the ground.

"Like a trench?"

"Yes, like a trench."

"Sarge, we got somewhere. Follow me and Ahmad."

They ran like crazy, diving into the fissure at the exact moment the first missile exploded barely one hundred meters away. There was more to come, much more. The Air Force had a flight of B-52Gs in the air, loaded for bear, and the bombs came crashing down like thunderbolts from hell, but infinitely deadlier. More bombs and missiles fell all around them, and all they could do was flatten themselves at the bottom of the trench.

Eddie had seen movies of the First World War in Europe, and he imagined it would have been like this. Men shivering with terror while thousands of tons of artillery dumped over their head, just meters away. Waiting for the end, for the crash of munitions exploding, and there would be oblivion as their lives were snatched from them.

It didn't happen. The barrage of bombs and missiles went on for hours, and it ended just before dawn. They poked their heads out of the trench, and the daylight exposed the devastation in its full, brutal destruction. The rolling landscape of low hills was transformed into a flattened wasteland, strewn with debris, broken weapons, bodies, and nearby, a wheel with the shreds of a rubber tire. All that remained of their Humvee.

"Jesus Christ," Dan murmured, "I can't believe we survived." He looked at Ahmad. "Kid, we owe you. You saved our lives."

He grinned self-consciously. "It is better to live than to die."

"Too right. So your Taliban days are over?"

"Yes, I have decided to fight a different war."

"A different war? What do you mean?"

"The game Call of Duty. There is no need for anyone to get killed."

He nodded. "Very wise. Eddie, we'll put in together and buy him what he needs. When we get back, fix it up."

"Sure thing, Sarge. He'll get the best." He looked at the Afghan boy. "One more thing you can do for me."

"What is that, Eddie?"

"Help me tote this machine gun. It's heavy."

They reached the track, and in the light of day they could see there was no ambush waiting for them. A column of vehicles arrived, and when the lead jeep stopped, a familiar figure leapt out. "You guys again, I might have known it. Did we get them all?"

Dan gestured to the lunar-like surface. "If any of them survived that little lot, they deserve to live."

His eyes widened. "Hot damn, those flyboys gave it a real pasting. Good work, all of you. Where's your vehicle?"

"The same place as those insurgents, Captain. In hell."

He smiled. "We'll get you another. I don't see Major McNally."

"He's dead, Sir. He took a bullet, and we thought he'd be okay, but they hit him again."

His face was grave. "I'm sorry, he was a good man, although he shouldn't have been out here. He was an Intelligence officer, not trained for this kind of thing. He was a brave man, coming out here. Maybe we should put him up for a medal."

"Yessir, maybe we should."

"Anyone else do especially well?"

Dan looked at Eddie, thought for a moment, and his gaze moved on. "Yessir, a new recruit, he did very well."

"What's his name?"

"Ahmad."

Rogers saw him then and did a double take. "An Afghan?"

"An Afghan, right."

"Can we give him a medal?"

"Kind of, Sir. But it's already taken care of."

The boy wasn't looking. His eyes were glued to the laptop screen, his hands moving on the keyboard and trackpad like he'd been doing it forever. Dan looked at Eddie. "You gave it to him?"

"He saved our lives, Sarge."

"He did that. When we get back, the priority is a new one for you. The latest and the best."

Eddie glanced at Ahmad. "You know what this means? We can go head to head."

The boy didn't understand the meaning, except it was something good.

Rogers looked puzzled, so he explained. "Better than him shooting at our men, Captain."

"Right. You did well, Hawkins, getting him on side. But I guess what matters is you had Major McNally leading you until the end."

"Yessir. Until the end."

Made in the USA
Columbia, SC
11 October 2022